Healthy & Fun Ways to Care for Your Body

Alex Kuskowski

Mishawaka-Penn-Harris
Public Library
Mishawaka, Indiana

visit us at www.abdopublishing.com

Published by ABDO Publishing Company, a division of ABDO, P.O. Box 398166, Minneapolis, Minnesota 55439. Copyright © 2013 by Abdo Consulting Group, Inc. International copyrights reserved in all countries. No part of this book may be reproduced in any form without written permission from the publisher. Checkerboard Library™ is a trademark and logo of ABDO Publishing Company.

Printed in the United States of America, North Mankato, Minnesota
062012
092012

 PRINTED ON RECYCLED PAPER

Design and Production: Mighty Media, Inc.
Series Editor: Liz Salzmann
Photo Credits: Colleen Dolphin, Shutterstock

The following manufacturers/names appearing in this book are trademarks: Aleene's®, Arm & Hammer ®, McCormick®, Sharpie®, The Original Super Glue®

Library of Congress Cataloging-in-Publication Data

Kuskowski, Alex.
  Cool body basics : healthy & fun ways to care for your body / Alex Kuskowski.
      p. cm. -- (Cool health and fitness)
  Audience: 8-12
  Includes bibliographical references and index.
  ISBN 978-1-61783-425-7 (alk. paper)
 1. Hygiene--Juvenile literature. I. Title.
 RA777.K87 2013
 613--dc23
                          2012010051

CONTENTS

Get Fresh!.. 4
Perfect Poise.. 6
Take Care!... 7
Make Time for You!....................................... 8
Cool Clean Center 10
Supplies 12
Totally Fresh Toothpaste 14
Marvelous Mirror.. 16
Zesty Orange Body Wash 18
Trendy Travel Toiletries................................ 20
Food for Thought 22
Clean Science.. 24
Drops of Mint... 28
Health Journal... 30
Glossary... 31
Web Sites... 31
Index 32

GET FRESH!

It's important to look and feel your best to make a good impression. You have to be aware of your body and not ignore its needs. Get up and take charge of keeping your body clean and healthy! Make your life fun and fresh.

There are a lot of great ways to clean up your act. Showering, washing your face, and being **confident** in yourself are all small things that can make a big difference. Try it out and strut your stuff. You'll love the new you!

Permission & Safety

- Always get **permission** before doing these activities.
- Always ask if you can use the tools, supplies, or gear you need.
- If you do something by yourself, make sure you do it safely.
- Ask for help when necessary.
- Be careful when using sharp objects.
- Make sure you're wearing the **appropriate** gear.

Be Prepared

- Read the entire activity before you begin.
- Make sure you have all the tools and materials listed.
- Do you have enough time to complete the activity?
- Keep your work area clean and organized.
- Follow the directions.
- Clean up any mess you make.

PERFECT POISE

Having *poise* means being and acting **confident** in yourself. This is easier to do when your body is clean and you feel fresh and healthy. Once you get started, you'll wonder why you weren't doing it all along.

All you have to do is find the right **routine** for you. Keeping healthy and clean is all about building it into your **schedule**. Make sure to eat right and exercise every day. Stay clean by washing up after you exercise.

COOL CONFIDENCE IN 1-2-3

> Stand and sit straight.

> When you're talking to someone look him or her in the eye.

> Smile! It will make everyone around you want to smile too.

TAKE CARE!

- Try something new. Get **confidence** from learning a new dance.

- Rest up. Getting enough sleep is an important part of being healthy. You need at least eight hours of sleep each night.

- Eat well. Your body needs the right **nutrition** for you to feel your best.

- Exercise. You'll feel energized and more confident.

- Wind down. Relax for you! You'll feel good inside and out.

- Wear sunscreen! Even on cloudy days it helps protect you from the sun's **dangerous** rays.

- Stay **hydrated**! Drink water. Put on lotion or moisturizer if your skin is dry or itchy.

MAKE TIME FOR YOU!

AROUND THE HOUSE (INSIDE)

Your home is the main place where you take care of your body. Try relaxing in a warm bath. You can read a magazine or listen to your favorite music.

AROUND THE HOUSE (OUTSIDE)

If you have nice weather you can enjoy the fresh air and space outside. You can go for a relaxing walk or have a picnic.

PLUGGED IN

Computers are used for a lot of things. Most kids use them for talking to friends and doing homework. But it can also help organize your body care **routine**. Type up what you do in the morning and at bedtime. Then you won't forget!

ON THE ROAD

Traveling can seem like it takes forever. It can be dirty too! Bring along your favorite soap from home to help you clean up when you arrive at your **destination**.

AT SCHOOL

Staying clean and **confident** at school is easy. Keep a mirror and brush in your locker. You can do a quick check between classes.

WITH FRIENDS

You can do so many fun things when you are playing with friends. Friends will always want to help you feel good! Get together with your friends and play your favorite game.

COOL CLEAN CENTER

CLEAN FACE!

Make sure you wash your face in the morning and before bed! Your face can get a lot of dirt on it. Washing your face also helps prevent pimples.

CLEAN TEETH!

Make sure you brush and floss your pearly whites every day. It'll keep your smile **confident** and bright! It will also keep your breath smelling fresh.

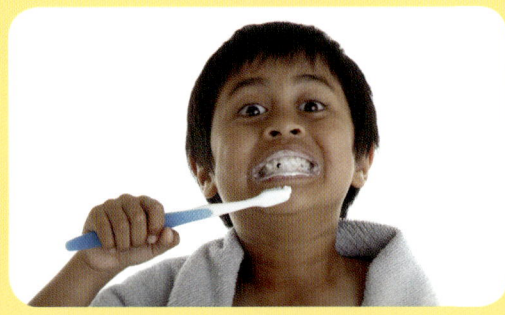

CLEAN BODY!

Take a shower or bath every day! It's important to wash your body and hair. Being clean helps you feel good and stay healthy.

CLEAN CLOTHES!

Clothes get dirty! Food or other things can spill on them. They can also get sweat and dirt on them when you exercise or play games. Wear clean clothes every day.

CLEAN HANDS!

Wash your hands often. And every time, make sure to rub them with the soap for at least 20 seconds. Make it fun! Sing a few lines of your favorite song while you wash.

SUPPLIES

Here are some of the things that you'll need to get started!

3-ounce plastic containers

acrylic paint

all-purpose permanent adhesive

baking soda

bottle with a pop-up squirt cap

clear sealant

craft glue

decorative gems

glass tiles

glitter glue

paint pens

peppermint extract

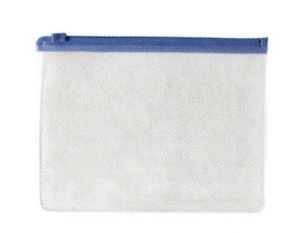
plastic travel case

puffy paint

seed beads

unscented shampoo or body wash

Totally Fresh Toothpaste

Brush tooth decay away!

WHAT YOU NEED

- 4 teaspoons baking soda
- ½ teaspoon salt
- 1 teaspoon peppermint extract
- measuring spoons
- mixing bowl
- spoon
- small container
- markers

1 Put the baking soda, salt, peppermint extract, and 1 teaspoon water in a mixing bowl. Stir the ingredients together until the mixture is a paste.

2 Put the mixture into the small container. Use markers to label the lid of the container.

3 When you brush your teeth, scoop out a little bit of the toothpaste with your toothbrush.

TIP: Try making toothpaste with different flavors! Use vanilla extract or almond extract.

15

Marvelous Mirror

 What a fantastic face!

WHAT YOU NEED

- mirror
- masking tape
- newspaper
- acrylic paint
- paintbrush
- all-purpose permanent adhesive
- glass tiles
- craft glue
- seed beads

1 If possible, remove the mirror from its frame. If the mirror cannot be removed, cover it with masking tape. Make sure you cover the edges all along the frame.

2 Set the frame on the newspaper. Paint the frame your favorite color. Let the paint dry. Add another coat of paint if necessary.

3 Use the permanent adhesive to glue glass tiles onto the frame. Put a dot of adhesive on a tile. Press it onto the frame. Hold it down for a few seconds. Then glue on the next tile.

4 For more decoration add small dots of craft glue. Sprinkle seed beads on the dots of glue.

5 When you are done, let the adhesive and craft glue dry completely. Then put the mirror back in the frame or remove the masking tape. Hang up the mirror and check your reflection!

TIP: Try making designs with the craft glue and beads. You could even write your name in glue and put beads on top!

Zesty Orange Body Wash

 Feel fresh and smell clean!

WHAT YOU NEED

- orange
- 2 cups unscented shampoo or body wash
- grater
- measuring spoons
- large bowl
- measuring cups
- mixing spoon
- funnel
- bottle with a pop-up squirt cap
- paint pens
- glitter glue
- decorative gems
- craft glue

1 Rub the outside of the orange on the grater to make orange zest. Rub only until the bright orange color disappears. Work your way around the orange until you have 3 tablespoons of orange zest. Put the zest in a large bowl.

2 Add ½ cup hot water. Let it sit for 10 minutes.

3 Add the unscented shampoo or body wash. Stir with a mixing spoon. Pour the mixture into a glass measuring cup.

4 Put the bottom of the funnel in the bottle. Pour the mixture into the top of the funnel. When the bottle is full, put the cap on.

5 Decorate the bottle with paint pens, glitter glue, and decorative gems.

6 Squeeze some into your hand whenever you need some **zesty** body wash!

TIP: Try using lemon zest instead of orange zest to get a different scent!

19

Trendy Travel Toiletries

 Add pizzazz to your trip!

WHAT YOU NEED

- newspaper
- 3 3-ounce plastic containers
- letter stickers
- plastic travel case
- puffy paint
- glitter glue
- decorative gems
- craft glue
- clear sealant

1 Cover your work area with newspaper. Label each plastic container using the letter stickers. Spell out "Soap," "Gel," "Cream," or anything else you want to bring.

2 Bling it up! Decorate the containers with puffy paint, glitter glue, and decorative gems.

3 Decorate the travel case too! Draw designs with puffy paint and glitter glue. Write your name or other words with letter stickers. Try gluing on decorative gems for extra sparkle.

4 Make sure the containers and travel case are lying on the newspaper. Spray them all with sealant. Let it dry according to the directions on the can.

AIRPLANE 3-1-1 POLICY

3 Liquids and gels have to be in containers that hold 3 ounces or less.

1 Put your containers of liquids and gels in a one-quart clear plastic zipper bag.

1 Each person can only carry on one bag of liquids and gels.

Food for Thought

 You are what you eat!

WHAT YOU NEED

- computer
- friend

1   Get together with a friend. Make a list of your favorite healthy foods. Be sure to include fruits and vegetables.

2   Next, pick one food to research on the computer. Your friend should do the same. Look up the **nutrition** facts about the food online. How many vitamins does it have? How much of it should you eat? Try to find as much information as you can.

3   When you are done researching your food, share what you learned with your friend. Your friend can tell you about what he or she learned too.

4   If you print out your research, put it in a binder to keep all of it together.

TIP: Look up a recipe that has your food as the main ingredient. Ask a parent if you can make the dish to share with your friend. Your friend may want to do the same with the food he or she researched.

JUNK FOOD

Food that is unhealthy is sometimes called junk food. A lot of junk food tastes really good. But the ingredients are very bad for your body. Junk food has a lot of fat, sugar, salt, and chemicals. Try to avoid eating junk food as much as you can!

Clean Science

 This epic experiment cleans up!

WHAT YOU NEED

- white T-shirt
- ruler
- marker
- scissors
- measuring spoons
- ketchup
- 3 small bowls
- measuring cup
- laundry detergent
- bleach
- 3 paper plates

1. Use a ruler to draw three 5-inch (10 cm) squares on the T-shirt. Cut them out.

2. Put ½ teaspoon of ketchup on each square. Let the ketchup dry overnight.

3. Put ½ cup of water in each of the bowls. Add 2 teaspoons of laundry detergent to one of the bowls. Add 2 teaspoons of bleach to another bowl. Leave one bowl with plain water.

4 Put one T-shirt square in each bowl. Scrub each square in its bowl. Make sure you wash your hands between bowls. Let the squares soak for 5 to 10 minutes.

5 While the squares are soaking, label the plates. Write "#1 Water" on one plate. Write "#2 Detergent" on the second plate. Write "#3 Bleach" on the third plate.

6 After they're done soaking, remove the squares from the bowls. Squeeze out the extra water.

7 Spread each square out on the plate that matches what was in its bowl. Compare the stains. Which method got the fabric the cleanest?

TIP: Try this experiment with different stains, such as juice or ink. Use different cleaners. See what works best!

Drops of Mint

 Fun fresh breath!

WHAT YOU NEED

- 4 ounces cream cheese
- 1 tablespoon softened butter
- 1 tablespoon light corn syrup
- ½ teaspoon peppermint extract
- 4 cups powdered sugar
- food coloring
- colored sprinkles
- baking sheet
- wax paper
- measuring spoons
- large mixing bowl
- hand mixer
- measuring cups
- drinking glass

1. Line the baking sheet with wax paper. Set it aside.

2. Put the cream cheese, butter, corn syrup, and peppermint extract in a large bowl. Mix with a hand mixer.

3. Slowly mix in the powdered sugar. Add a little bit at a time until all the powdered sugar is mixed in.

4. Add a few drops of food coloring. Mix in the food coloring with the hand mixer. You can add more drops until it's the color you want.

5. Roll the mixture into ½-inch (1.3 cm) balls. Put the balls on the cookie sheet.

6. Flatten each ball with the bottom of a drinking glass

7. Put colored sprinkles on top to make them extra sweet! Store them in the refrigerator.

Health Journal

Try keeping a health and fitness journal! Write down your morning and bedtime cleaning **routines**. Record other times during the day you do something good for your body. This makes it easy to look back and see how you are keeping your body clean and healthy. It could also show you where there's room for improvement. Decorate your journal to show your personal style!

Glossary

appropriate – suitable, fitting, or proper for a specific occasion.

confident – sure of one's self and one's abilities.

dangerous – able or likely to cause harm or injury.

destination – the place where you are going to.

hydrated – having enough water or moisture.

nutrition – how different foods affect one's health.

permission – when a person in charge says it's okay to do something.

routine – a regular order of actions or way of doing something.

schedule – a list of the times when things will happen.

zesty – having a lively, spicy flavor or scent.

Web Sites

To learn more about health and fitness for kids, visit ABDO Publishing Company online at www.abdopublishing.com. Web sites about ways for kids to stay fit and healthy are featured on our Book Links page. These links are routinely monitored and updated to provide the most current information available.

Index

A
Airplanes, taking liquids and gels on, 21

B
Body, washing of, 11
Body wash, activity for making, 18–19
Breath mints, activity for making, 28–29

C
Clean body, importance of, 4, 6
Clothes, cleanliness of, 11
Computer
  activity using, 22–23
  health and fitness using, 9
Confidence, ways to develop, 6–7

E
Exercise, importance of, 6, 7

F
Face, washing of, 10
Friends
  activity with, 22–23
  health and fitness with, 9

H
Hair, washing of, 11
Hands, washing of, 11

Healthy body, importance of, 4, 6
Home, health and fitness at, 8

J
Journal, for health and fitness, 30
Junk food, 23

M
Mirror, activity for making, 16–17

N
Nutrition
  activity for planning, 22–23
  importance of, 6, 7

O
Outdoors, health and fitness in, 8

P
Permission, for doing activities, 5
Poise, 6
Preparing, to do activities, 5

R
Relaxing, importance of, 7, 8
Routines, for being clean and healthy, 6, 30

S
Safety, in doing activities, 5
Schedule, and being clean and healthy, 6
School, health and fitness at, 9
Skin care, 7, 10
Sleep, importance of, 7
Stain removal, activity for, 24–27
Supplies, for doing activities, 5, 12–13

T
Teeth, brushing and flossing of, 10
Toiletries, activity for making, 20–21
Toothpaste, activity for making, 14–15
Traveling
  health and fitness during, 9
  toiletries for, 20–21

W
Web sites, about health and fitness, 31